WISDOM
of
PANDAS

Compiled by
Franchesca Ho Sang

HYLAS

Hylas Publishing®
129 Main Street, Ste. C
Irvington, NY 10533
www.hylaspublishing.com

Hylas Publishing
Publisher: Sean Moore
Publishing Director: Karen Prince
Art Director: Gus Yoo
Designer: La Tricia Watford
Editor: Franchesca Ho Sang
Proofreader: Suzanne Lander

ISBN: 1-59258-253-2
ISBN 13/EAN: 978-1592-58253-2

Library of Congress Cataloging-in-Publication Data available upon request.
Printed and bound in Singapore
Distributed in the United States by Publishers Group West
Distributed in Canada by Publishers Group Canada
First American Edition published in 2006

2 4 6 8 10 9 7 5 3 1

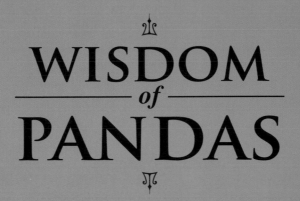

WISDOM
of
PANDAS

Compiled by
Franchesca Ho Sang

www.hylaspublishing.com

"Bite off more
than you can chew,
then chew it."

"As we are **liberated** from our own fear, our **presence** automatically **liberates** others."

–Nelson Mandela

"When what we are
is what we want to be,
that's happiness."

–*Malcolm S. Forbes*

"Follow your instincts. That's where true wisdom manifests itself."

–Oprah Winfrey

"The **well-run group** is not a **battlefield** of egos."

–*Lao Tzu*

"When **life** knocks
you down, **try to land**
on your **back**.
Because if you can look up,
you can get up."

–Les Brown

"**Hold fast
to dreams**,
for if dreams
die life is a
broken winged
bird that
cannot fly."

–*Langston Hughes*

"Success is falling
nine times
and getting up ten."

–Jon Bon Jovi

"There is
nothing better
than the
encouragement
of a good
friend."

–Katharine Hathaway

"Every **great dream** begins with **a dreamer.**"

–Harriet Tubman

"It is not so much our friends' help that helps us as the **confident knowledge** that they will help us."

–*Epicurus*

"The art of becoming wise
is the art of knowing
what to overlook."

–William James

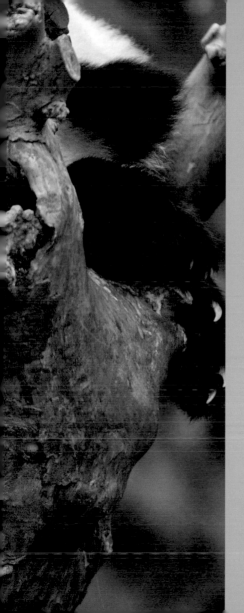

"**A good
laugh** and
a **long sleep**
are the
best cures in
the doctor's
book."

–Irish proverb

"The first step
towards amendment
is the recognition
of error."

–Seneca

"Fearless minds climb soonest into crowns."

–Shakespeare

"Life must be lived
and curiosity kept alive."

–Eleanor Roosevelt

"Discovery consists of looking at the same thing as everyone else and thinking some different."

–*Albert Szent-Gyogi*

"**Opportunity** often **comes in** the form of **misfortune** or temporary **defeat**."

–Napoleon

"It doesn't matter
how slowly you go
as long as you
do not stop."

–*Confucius*

"In order **to understand** the world, one has to **turn away** from it on occasion."

–*Albert Camus*

"It's never too late to be who you might have been."

–*George Eliot*

"Concentration is the secret of strenth."

–*Ralph Waldo Emerson*

"The most wasted of all days is the one without laughter."

–*E.E. Cummings*

"Improvement makes straight roads; but the crooked roads without improvement are roads of genius."

–*William Blake*

"Every step of life
shows much caution
is required."

–*Goethe*

"**Imagination is** more important than **knowledge**."

–Albert Einstein

"We may encounter many defeats, but we must not be defeated."

–*Maya Angelou*

"Greatness does not approach him who is forever looking down."

–Hitopadesa

"Kites **rise highest** against the wind, **not with it.**"

–*Winston Churchill*

"Look back,
and smile at perils past."

–Sir Walter Scott

"Peace begins
with a smile."

–*Mother Teresa*

"By seeking and
blundering we learn."

–*Goethe*

"Beauty in things exists in the mind which contemplates them."

–David Hume

"At the innermost core
of all **loneliness**
is a deep and
powerful yearning
for **union** with
one's self."

–Brendan Francis

"Too often we…enjoy the comfort of opinion without the discomfort of thought."

–*John F. Kennedy*

"Subdue your appetites, my dears, and you've conquered human nature."

–*Charles Dickens*

"Think **big thoughts** but, relish **small pleasures.**"

–*H. Jackson Brown, Jr.*

"A **closed mind** is like a closed book;
just a **block of wood**.

−*Chinese proverb*

"One who does
not look ahead
remains behind."

–*Brazilian proverb*

"Our **envy** of others
devours us most of **all**."

–Alexander Solzhenitsyn

"**In** the middle of **difficulty lies opportunities.**"

–*Albert Einstein*

"Spend time alone everyday."

–Dalai Lama

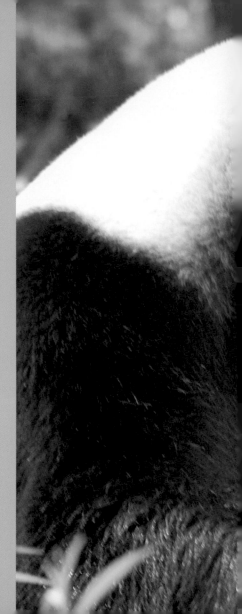

"The **art** of **being happy** lies in the power of **extracting** happiness from **common things.**"

–Henry Ward Beecher

"If you can find a **path** with **no obstacles**, it probably **doesn't lead anywhere**."

–Frank A. Clark

"Love the whole world as a mother loves her only child."

–Buddha

"Hunger is the handmaid of genius."

–*Mark Twain*

"**Success** is
to be **measured**
not so much **by**
the position
that one has
reached in life…
as by the
obstacles which
he has **overcome**
while trying to
succeed."

–*Booker T. Washington*

"Society is a masked ball, where everyone hides his real character, and reveals it by hiding."

–Ralph Waldo Emerson

"**Live** and **work but do not** forget to play, to have fun in life and really enjoy it."

–*Eileen Caddy*

"Be so **strong** that nothing can disturb your **peace** of mind."

–*Christian Larson*

"In **wisdom** gathered **over time** I have found that **every experience is** a form of **exploration.**"

–Ansel Adams

"He who leaves
his house in search
of happiness
pursues a shadow."

—*Anonymous*

"Satisfaction
lies in the
effort, not
in the the
attainment.
**Full effort is
full victory.**"

–*Ghandi*

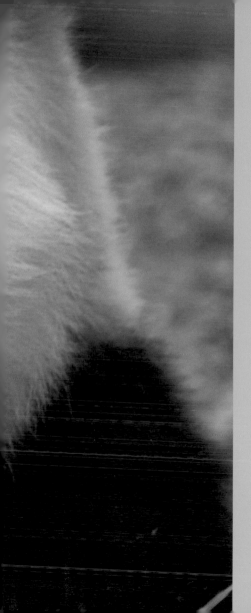

"The bashful
are always
aggressive
at heart."

–Charles Horton Cooley

"Knowing others is wisdom, knowing yourself is enlightenment."

–Lao Tzu

"Sometimes your **joy** is the source of your smile, but sometimes your smile can be the source of your joy."

–*Thich Nhat Hanh*

"Find **ecstasy in life**; the mere sense of **living is joy** enough."

–*Emily Dickinson*

PICTURE CREDITS